THE ADIRONDACK PRINCESS BOOK II

THE ADIRONDACK PRINCESS BOOK II

An Historical Novel

by

Doris E. Schuyler

Published by
Canal Side Publishers
3517 State Route Five
Schuyler, NY 13340

Printed In U.S.A.
by Steffen Press
Holland Patent, N.Y.

Other works by the author:
The Adirondack Princess 1982
Aunt Cad 1984
Butlersbury 1985

Library of Congress Catalog Number 90-83639
ISBN 0-9628208-0-6

Dedication

to Will, Robert and John
with love

Preface

Confronted with a tragic fire which destroyed her home and separated her from her family, our heroine was rescued by a handsome Indian brave.

She fell in love, and the outcome presented us with a new concept of the Indians.

They were found to be thoughtful, kind and creative survivors.

The saga continues at the point where we left them in "The Adirondack Princess," with Emmie at their trading post.

THE ADIRONDACK PRINCESS
BOOK II

CHAPTER I

Emmie was roused from deep thought by a hand on her shoulder. She knew, without turning or looking up, that it was Luke's hand; no one else, she was sure, had such a strong, yet gentle, tender touch.

Ever since Ellen had married and gone to live in New York City, Emmie had taken to sitting on the new porch in the afternoon and watching the traffic on the canal. "Traffic" was a new word upstate, where, before the canal, a wagon or two a day on the trails had been the extent of the travel one could expect.

The canal had changed a great many things in the lives of the upstaters, or, Emmie thought, for that matter, in the lives of a great many other folks, too. People who had only dreamed of going west now crammed the packets day after day, some carrying only those possessions that could be packed in a pack, hoping for a new beginning in the west. Many had arrived in this new world as indentured servants, and had served their masters well, and had earned the right to strike out on their own, and were now off to seek their own fortune.

Emmie and Luke were well aware of this situation, for many of the travelers had only enough money to pay their fare to the lock station just east of the Post, and these people often camped behind the Inn, and hired out to Luke for a few days to earnenough to pay their fare around the lake to the next station, and in that way, they would work themselves and their families toward their goals.

Luke was very worried about his Princess. Ellen had taken the place in their hearts of the child they never had, and now that she had married and moved away, he felt he and Emmie must find something new or different to occupy their thoughts and energies. Emmie still kept the ledgers for both the Post and the Inn, but the O'Donnell and the O'Neil women had taken over most of the other chores. Even the children of these families helped when needed, and, of course, extra help from stranded travelers was always plentiful.

Emmie's thoughts were not only of the future, but also of the past. In fact, her thoughts went back to the fire which had not only destroyed her father's farm buildings, but had taken the lives of her mother and all the farm animals--of how she had run to the cave by the river to escape death herself, and then had swum to the north shore, and had run into the mountains trying to escape she knew not what. Her fear and dread of the Indians? Of wild animals? She could not remember her aches, bruises, cuts and scrapes, but she did remember Luke--that handsome young Indian lad that rescued her, and took her to his people who accepted her, and healed her wounds, and how Luke had healed the dreadful ache in her heart with his love for her; and of his father, the Old Chief, tired and crippled with age, allowing his son and heir to marry her and leave the family compound to go with her and learn and live the ways of the White Man. And she thought of their cabin and little farm in the mountains, of the long lonely nights when Luke would be off tending his trap line, and how they struggled together. Luke learning from her and she from him. And there was Ebony, her very own horse, a gift from the Old Chief, and how many trips they had made up and down the mountain together; and how, on her first trip back to the valley, she had been befriended, not only by Maria Swenson and her family, but also by the Beckers. The elderly childless couple who owned the trading post. They had taken her in their home as their own, and how, after many trips she had brought Luke to meet all of her friends, the people she called her new family.

She was recalling how Violet, the young Indian maiden, had come to live with she and Luke; how the young brave, Joseph, had come to woo Violet, and take her back to the family compound, but instead, had married her and taken over the little farm so that she and Luke could go to the valley and be with the aging Mrs. Becker and run the trading post after Mr. Becker had died.

These things were all part of Emmie's thoughts as she sat day after day on the new porch and tried to decide with Luke their future and the future of the Post.

Summer seemed to end abruptly that year, with cold east winds bringing frost early in September. The wome folk were kept unusually busy preparing and preserving the garden produce that had to be hurriedly gathered so as not to be ruined by the frost. The gardens had been greatly enlarged in the spring to produce enough to supply the Inn and the three families, and now more storage space was needed for the extra crops.

The O'Donnells and the O'Neils had suggested what they called a "root cellar," and had dug a great pit in the knoll behind the Inn. They then cut logs to cover this hole, and covered the logs with dirt and sod. An entrance way was fashioned by placing planks, leading in a ramp-like fashion to the front side of the pit. The children were set to gathering dried leaves, and the potatoes, beets, carrots and turnips were laid in bins of leaves, and covered with dried sand. The other vegetables, such as onions and squash, were strung and hung from the ceiling planks. Emmie did not help, but thought through all this hustle and bustle, how very much their lives had changed since they had taken over the Post. When she and Luke had come to the valley, the Swenson's were then their nearest neighbors, a hard ride of half a day away, and were, outside of the Becker's, the only persons that they knew personally, and there weeks on end, after Mr. Becker died and Mrs. Becker had left, that the only persons besides themselves that they saw or talked to (except for the busy spring and fall trading) was a lone traveler or hunter, and Old Jake and his squaw.

CHAPTER II

When Joseph arrived from the mountains, he had much the same tale of the early frost, but unlike the O'Donnells and O'Neils, had lost a lot of their crops. He carried a letter from Violet to Emmie, and she retreated to the privacy of their living quarters to read it. She smiled as she opened the folded paper, thinking of her first paper and charcoal pencil, and of teaching Violet to write. The first part of the letter was general news of life on the little farm, and of a recent visit to the tribal compound, and then the real purpose of writing the letter surfaced. Violet wanted her children to spend the winter with Emmie and Luke at the Post and Inn, and she was asking Emmie to teach them the things she had taught her; writing and numbers and reading. She went on to say that she had taught them all she could, and training others did not come easy to either she or Joseph, for all Joseph's training had come from Violet. Emmie felt that this would be a tremendous responsibility. She, herself, had no real formal education, and she sadly recalled Papa teasingly chiding Ma about too much "l'arnin'" when she was a child , and Ma was teaching herself and the boys in the bright, friendly kitchen so long ago. She carefully refolded the letter and put it on the mantle. This was a request she would have to give some further thought to.

Luke and Emmie ate most of their main meals at the Inn. There was always plenty of food,and they both liked the company the dining room provided. They had gotten into this habit when Ellen left, and it seemed a good arrangement to everyone. But Emmie was aware of Joseph's shyness with strangers, and so decided to cook supper in her own kitchen tonight. She worked steadily all afternoon in the kitchen, leaving the Post to Luke and Joseph, and by the time the men had finished getting materials on Joseph's list together, Emmie had a delightful meal ready for them. Luke teased her a little about not having lost her touch in the kitchen, and the meal passed with light conversation between them about the farm and Violet. After they had eaten, Luke and Joseph went out on the porch with their pipes, and although Emmie could have called one of the O'Neil children to clear away the food and do the dishes, and join them, she chose to do the work herself - herself, because she needed even more time to think alone about the request in Violet's letter. Joseph would be starting back up the mountains early in the morning, and she must decide what her answer would be. She wanted to talk it over with Luke before making any final decision. As soon as they had finished their pipes, the men came in as the night air had a distinct chill about it, and Joseph immediately said good-night and retired. Without Violet, he felt shy among his friends, and he wanted to rest as long as possible, for he had ridden hard, and must face the same long ride returning up the mountain to the farm tomorrow.

Luke touched off the log that

had been laid in the living room fireplace, and he and Emmie sat cross-legged on the floor, as they often did, and watched the fire as they warmed themselves before going to bed.

Emmie went to the kitchen and brought back two large mugs of hot tea and the letter from Violet. After she read the letter aloud to Luke, they sat in silence for several minutes. It was Luke who spoke first, and with great enthusiasm he said the he thought that Violet had a real fine plan, and that they should help her. The Post was still a busy place in the spring and fall, even with the canal in operation, and shipping and buying was made so much easier, but in the winter life could become very quiet and he thought having the young folks around would be a good thing.

So, with no more discussion, Emmie got out her paper and pen and wrote their answer to Violet. Joseph left early in the morning. The sun was just breaking over the horizon, and it promised a clear fall day for his ride up the mountains. He no longer followed the river and crossed the swamplands by the Swenson's, but followed an old trail that went directly north just a few yards west of the Post, and saved a great deal of time. This was a much steeper trail, but his load was comparatively light, and so he was up and away before Emmie was up. She was sorry to have missed him, but Luke assured her that he had carried the letter for Violet safely with him.

There had been no times or dates set for the children's arrival, and Emmie was surprised when they arrived within a week. The only preparations she had made were in her mind, and so there seemed to be complete confusion everywhere for the first few days. Violet, Emmie knew, had worked hard at getting the children ready to spend the winter away from home. The boy had fine leather trousers and shirts, and the girl had two fine leather tunics. One, Emmie thought, quite like the one the Indians had made for her wedding those many years ago. They also had leggings and moccasins and warm fur outerwraps to complete their wardrobe.

They had been there but a few days, after getting acquainted with the O'Donnell and O'Neil children, when Emmie decided that their Indian garb made them too conspicuous , and so preparations were laid for new outfits. Emmie reminisced to herself for a few minutes as she sat on her porch that afternoon. On her first trip to the valley, after having lived in the mountains for so long, she had worn her very best (wedding) Indian dress, and here she was, making clothes for Violet's children so they would not look so "Indian-ish."

Emmie had just taken it for granted that she would hold her classes in the kitchen as Ma had done with her and her brothers, but after the children arrived and had become acquainted with the O'Donnell and O'Neil children, and she learned that they were all interested in classes, she spoke to Luke about using the small dining room at the Inn. And so, just one week after Violet's children, Teka and Little Luke had arrived, Emmie held her first class. The children were anxious to learn, and that, Emmie thought years later, was her saving grace. She had had no formal education, only what Ma had taught her and what she had learned through experience and trial and error over the years. She had no set plans when they started classes, and no equipment such as readers and manuals, so the first few weeks passed with no rigid rules, and mostly just getting better acquainted with each other, and the use of slates and pencils, adjusting to life and the White Man's ways in the valley, and the White Man's language. Violet had taught them the small vocabulary she had picked up from Emmie and Luke several years ago, but had, herself, regressed to her native tongue when they had left and progress seemed very slow to Emmie.

One thing Emmie had learned since the opening of the canal was that news traveled up and down the valley much more rapidly than ever before imagined, and some of the news of her little classes came back to her, and the return word was more fancy than true. With one of the last boats before the canal would close for the winter came several salesmen, all wanting to sell Emmie readers and slates and classroom equipment. She was thoroughly overcome by the many books and manuals that they showed her. Time was growing short, and if the men were to return by the canal, she must make some decisions. One of the men whom Emmie felt more inclined to deal with than any of the others she invited to take the evening meal with she and Luke in their home, thinking it would be less confusing than at the Inn. Thre were several questions she wanted to clarify with him about quantities and shipments overland.

As they finished their meal and were about to begin their business, he drew out a gold watch, and carefully opening the case, checked the time, and as he did so, a strange feeling came over Emmie. She was remembering times, many years ago. when she had seen someone do exactly the same thing after the evening meal. The memories became very clear to her, and she felt herself in another kitchen, watching not only the same procedure, but seeing the exact same watch.

CHAPTER III

The young man looked up at Emmie, and noting the look on her face, hesitated before replacing the watch in his pocket. but no words passed between them about the incident.

Emmie decided on a reader and a large slate that Luke could fasten to the wall at the head of the classroom, and after some small talk, the salesman returned to his room at the Inn.

As she and Luke sat silently before the fireplace, Emmie's thoughts kept returning to the watch, and suddenly she jumped up and clapped her hands, and turning to Luke, she loudly shouted, "I know! I know!"

Luke was most confused over her actions, and tried to calm her and ask questions at the same time. What was it that she so suddenly knew?

"Where I have seen the gold watch that the young salesman had?" she said. She finally made him understand that her father had had a watch exactly like that one, and had always checked the watch after the evening meal. It was then that she realized that she had not known the young man's name, only the company that he represented. Could it be her brother? Who else would have her father's watch - if it really was the watch she remembered as a young child?

Luke tried to explain to her the many reasons he could think of why the watch was just one very similar to the one she remembered. After all, it had been many, many years since she had seen the watch, and surely she could not think the man to be her brother, for he was such a young man. Luke recalled her tales of her brothers being much older that herself. And so, after little more discussion, they retired to a restless, sleepless night.

As the first rays of light appeared in the east, Emmie was up and dressing. She had thought a thousand times through the night just how she would ask the young man about his watch. Should she just ask right out about its origin, or what should she do? She and Luke walked over to the Inn and joined the young man for breakfast, and Emmie could not contain herself, and so immediately asked his full name. He had introduced himself as Chris, from the Acme Book Company, and she suggested that she would like to know more about him and his background. He did not seem the least startled, but instead, offered an apology for not having divulged more about himself the day before. His name, he said, was Christopher Van der Veer, and that he lived with his parents in New York City. His father, he said, had lived in the Upper Mohawk Valley as a young man, but due to some tragedy that he, Chris, was not quite sure of, had come to the city and had been an apprentice printer for some time, and had eventually bought an interest in the business, and now that Chris had completed his schooling, he had been hired by the company as a salesman. He had chosen selling over printing because he wanted to travel, and he thought combiningtravel with work would be a fine opportunity for a young man.

He seemed interested in relating all this to Emmie and Luke, and continued with his story, not seeming to notice that Both Emmie and Luke had turned a ghostly white at the mention of the name Van der Veer. He went on to relate to them that upon his graduation from the Academy where he had studied. that his grandfather had given him his most prized possession, the gold watch, which he carried with him.

Tears rolled down Emmie's cheeks. Her father's watch! She was too overcome with emotion to speak, and Luke, sensing the situation, took over for her, starting with the announcement that Emmie, his wife, was christened Emmaline Van der Veer, and that he suspected that there could be a connection between the two families. From that point on, the conversation, to anyone listening, would no doubt had sounded boisterous and exuberant, but of course that was only because all three of them were trying to talk and ask questions at the same time.

The hour for opening the Post came and went as the three talked on and on. It was not until they were greeted by great shouting from some traders, asking who ran the Post, where were they? that they realized how long they had talked. Luke left Emmie and Chris to further sift through their family remembrances, and excused himself to go an open the Post and get on with the business at hand.

The young man could not believe that he had found his father's sister. He had never even known that such a person existed. His father never spoke of anyone except his uncle, who was also a member of the Acme firm, and his grandfather, about whose past he knew very little except that he had been a trader of sorts until his poor health had forced him into retirement. The tragic fire had seldom been spoken of, and because of the deep silences that surrounded the seldom-mention subject, he had never felt free to ask.

He was delighted with all the information about his family that Emmie was imparting, and it was noon before they had hardly paused for breath. The children had all left the schoolroom when Emmie had failed to appear in the morning, and had taken the opportunity to go to the river and fish--all except Jean O'Donnell, who had gone to the woods and was busy gathering nuts.

Chris was now very anxious to return to New York and tell his father the news that Emmie was alive and well, and so, with orders for books and slate in hand, and his head reeling with information and messages from his newfound aunt, he boarded the last packet for Albany on the first leg of his journey home.

CHAPTER IV

Life must go on, Emmie rationalized, but how could she settle down to teaching with her head and heart so full of the news she had just learned? Luke suggested that even though the weather was very cool, he and Emmie take a ride over to the Swenson's the next morning. Mrs. O'Donnell could tend the Post. Business was slowing up considerably, and with no boats in the canal, and very little overland travel, they could, perhaps, arrange to be away for a few days. Emmie felt small pangs of guilt at leaving the children, as they were just starting to settle down into a routine, but it took little urging on Luke's part to convince her. Maria knew the story of the tragic fire, and how Emmie had hoped against hope that somehow, some day, she would hear some news of her father and brothers.Luke, she knew, would enjoy a visit with George Swenson, and the change would be good for both of them.

Ebony was getting very, very old, with gray streaking his silky mane, and Emmie seldom rode him any more. He spent most of his days pasturing and sunning in the pasture just east of the Post. But Luke had brought him around with his horse for Emmie to ride to Maria's. He felt that Emmie needed the familiarity of Ebony beneath her in her excited state of mind. Emmie still rode astride and bareback, even though it was most unfashionable in the valley in these changing times.

The ride west to the Swenson's farm used to take nearly all of the daylight hours, but now the trail was much wider and more firmly packed, skirting the marshy fields, and the horses could trot along much faster, and even with their late start they were in sight of the farm long before the sun had begun to set . Jon was in the north pasture, fixing fences, and he recognized them and waved and shouted as they rounded the bend around the lowlands. His shoulders were broad, and he was taller than George, and as they drew closer, Emmie could see his chest heave and the muscles of his forearms bulge as he swung the heavy maul to drive in the new posts. She glanced at Luke beside her and knew he was remembering the little boy he had met on his first trip to the farm from the Post. He called to Emmie, and was off in a flash, across the meadow to talk with Jon.

Emmie rode on the last few rods alone, but Maria and George had heard the shouting and were in the dooryard to greet her. The old friends were glad they had come, and after their greeting, Maria and Emmie went into the big friendly kitchen. George, after taking care of Ebony, saddled his own horse to ride out to the meadow to greet Luke, and before too long, they were all gathered around the big table having cookies and tea.

Suddenly, not being able to contain herself any longer, Emmie blurted out her news. Words tumbled from her lips so fast that her tale was not coherent. Finally, Luke put his hand on her shoulder and made his Indian sign for "quiet." With his arm around her, he slowly and deliberately related the story of the book salesman and the gold watch. When he finished, they sat in silence, with tears of joy running over the cheeks of all, even George and Jon. Maria was the first to move or speak, and she rose and stepped around the table and clasped Emmie to her breast, and they clung together for several minutes.

Jon, having been born long after the tragic fire, had never heard the story of Emmie's life. She had always been Luke's wife ever since he could remember, and he had always just accepted her as such, never questioning, only accepting, and as he now looked around at his parents and Luke and Emmie, he knew instinctively what an important event this was, and he withdrew to a bunk beside the kitchen fireplace, not to eavesdrop, but to listen and learn the life story of his friends. As the tale unwound, he learned of the fire; of Emmie's escape into the hills; of how Luke found her and took her to his people; and after her physical wounds were healed, they were wed and she and Luke left the compound of his family and the ways of his ancestors to follow with Emmie, the ways of the White Man.

The only blot on Emmie's happiness all these long years had been not only the loss of her mother in the fire, but the ever-nagging thought of what her father and brothers had thought and done when they had returned home. And now, after these many, many years, Emmie had found the answers to the questions that had always, even in her happiest moments, troubled her.

They chatted right through the evening meal, and long past their regular bedtime, but when they finally did retire, sleep came almost instantly.

Emmie and Luke had the loft that hadn't been used since Ellen had left. Jon had grown too tall to stand up in the low space, and had built for himself the bunk beside the fireplace.

The loft was clean and quiet, and with Maria's beautiful soft and warm quilts, they slept well. The weather on their ride to the Swenson's had been through brisk breezes, but the household awoke to an entirely different day. Snow had started falling shortly after they had retired, and many inches of soft, white cloud-like drifts confronted Jon and George as they started for the barn, and by the time Maria had the kitchen fire up, and water boiling for coffee, the storm had increased and she could hardly make out the barn and sheds as she peered out the kitchen window. They all knew it would be foolhardy for Emmie and Luke to even try to make it back to the Post and Inn under such conditions, and so they settled in to wait for the storm to abate.

Emmie and Maria would never be visited out, and with the excitement of meeting her nephew, and the prospect of being reunited in the spring with her father and brothers, she and Maria speculated for hours. They wondered what they would be like now, after all these years; and about what she should wear when they met, and what they would have to say to each other. She was no longer their little sister, or her father's baby, which he had insisted she was, even at 16. Never in her wildest dreams did it ever occur to Emmie that they might not accept Luke. He had saved her from certain death, his people had healed her wounds, and when they had returned to the valley, he had taken her name--surely they would accept him as a son and brother.

While Emmie and Maria chatted and cooked, they found time after the evening meal for hand work. Emmie helping Maria to quilt some blocks she was readying for a Christmas gift for Ellen and Mr. Wilson. Luke, George and Jon spent hours shoveling their way back and forth to the barn.

The animals had to be fed and watered and the stalls cleaned, the cows milked and the eggs gathered. After each expedition to the outside, they would return, looking like walking snow-men; covered from head to toe with the fine, white snow that continued to fall.

The storm raged for two days, and on the third day, when the sun finally popped out from behind the clouds, and the winds had subsided, they found that the snowdrifts were numerous and high. It would be an almost impossible task to get the horses through the drifts, and they would need heavier clothing, as with the end of the snowfall, the temperature had plummeted, and the sting of the cold winds was biting indeed. They all knew that the O'Donnells could take care of the

Post and Inn, but never having been away together longer than a few days, they were anxious to return. And so, after a hearty breakfast, and bundled up in borrowed clothes, they started off. While they had been waiting for the storm to subside, the men had busied themselves with odd jobs in the barn between regular chores, and Luke had found some old snow-shoe frames. He repaired them with strips of rawhide from a skin Jon had cured from a bull calf they had slaughtered in the early summer. It took little persuasion to add them to their packs.

The going was very slow. In order to avoid huge drifts, they had to detour off the trail. This was very tiring for their horses and also very time-consuming, and in some instances, almost doubling the mileage of the old trail. Ebony tired easily, and they stopped many times to ease his load and rest him. It was well past noon when they stopped for a quick snack. Emmie was sorry not to be able to take more time, and soon the fine lunch that Maria had packed was eaten. But the elements were not on their side, and haste was a necessity now. After they had eaten, Luke put on the snowshoes and had Emmie ride his horse so that Ebony would be better able to keep up the struggling pace.

It was obvious that they would not be able to make it home by nightfall, with drifts obscuring the trail, and the slow pace of Ebony they decided, just before sundown, that they must make a camp and rest for the night. With the snowshoes for shovels they dug into the side of a drift, fashioning a makeshift shelter. Luke spread a blanket over the few boughs he had been able to gather nearby, and they settled in to wait for darkness to pass. Their horses were uneasy, but they knew that their pacing back and forth was keeping them from getting too cold. Neither slept, but huddled together in the little shelter, and when the sun appeared all were ready to proceed.

They realized, after just a short distance, that they had passed the halfway mark. As they worked their way east, they found that the storm had not been nearly so severe, and traveling became much easier, but even so, it was well past sundown when the lights of the Inn were spotted in the distance. It was a welcome sight indeed. They went directly to the Inn and were greeted like royalty. The Inn was filled to capacity with stranded travelers, and even the youngest O'Donnell had been pressed into kitchen and dining room service. A huge kettle of Mrs. O'Donnell's hearty Irish stew was steaming on the great fireplace crane, and Emmie and Luke partook ravishingly. After they were thoroughly warmed and fed, and could see that everything at the Inn was nicely under control, they walked to their house and the Post. The fires had much earlier been banked for the night, but the rooms were still warm. As Emmie readied herself for bed she realized how very tired she was, and she thought she might sleep for several days.

CHAPTER V

The children were waiting for her when she walked across the lane to the Inn the next morning, and were anxious to get back to their studies. The few days they had had to frolic in the snow were over, and they were ready to settle down. They advanced rapidly, especially the older boys, and Emmie knew that even with the aid of the books that she would soon have to teach from, by spring they would have advanced beyond her ability to teach them further.

The winter weather continued to be very unsettled, with heavy snowfalls and short thaws causing the men great concern over the strength of the roofs, and several times they had had to climb up on the Inn roof and remove the snow. It was ever a source of amazement to Emmie that the elements could be the cause of such consternation. The great banks of snow shielded them from the icy blasts of wind, and yet could cause such problems if in the wrong place.

For weeks there were no travelers except for a trapper or two seeking shelter, and a few who needed supplies. The east and west winds kept the canal ice quite free from snow, and the children delighted in sliding. On days when the sun was bright and the air crisp, Emmie would dismiss class early so that they might enjoy their sport.

With the coming of spring, many things besides the weather began to change. As the canal opened once again for commerce, and more and more settlers came to the valley, the little settlements became villages, and the villages became cities.

Both Emmie and Luke realized that the Post was no longer a thriving trading post for the trappers and hunters whose furs and hides were being purchased on the spot by traveling agents from the large fur companies thathad developed in New York City and Philadelphia. Under the general consensus of opinion they decided they would fare better with actual cash deals than trading. The farms were growing larger, and help easier to come by, as both young men and young women worked their way to the great western plains, an opportunity opened to them by the Erie Canal. They also realized that the farmers were shipping more and more grain and food stuffs to the larger cities in the east. So the trading post would either have to change with the times or shut down completely.

After many evenings of pros and cons they decided that a general store would be more profitable and meet the needs of the settlers and travelers alike. The Inn was thriving, and it was decided that the space used for the school should be turned back to dining room space. Through the summer months they could build a small building,expressly for a school. As the time neared for spring plowing and planting to begin, Emmie dismissed her pupils so that they might help with these chores.

The ponies that Teka and Little Luke rode in on in the fall

had been well fed and cared for, and had grown considerably, and seemed anxious to be ridden. So as soon as the spring floods had subsided, the children set out to return to their parents and the little farm in the mountains. Their heads full of knowledge, and their bodies clothed in the garb of the White Man. They both asked to take their slates and pencils and readers with them, that they might continue their studies at home, and promised to return in the fall.

CHAPTER VI

Emmie had no time to be lonesome after dismissing school that spring, for besides converting the Post into a fullfledged general store, she was preparing for a visit from her brothers and their families.

Letters from Ellen had conveyed the grandeur of city life. The exquisite furnishings of the homes, and the lifestyle that businessmen and tradesmen enjoyed was far above what she and Luke thought of a luxurious here in the foothills of the great mountains and the valley of their great river. But Emmie, remembering her first winter in the

Indian compound, and later on the little mountain farm, was tremendously happy with the life-style she and Luke now enjoyed, and she went about her spring cleaning chores with a song in her heart, preparing for her visitors until the rider brought the letter from her brother that was to change all this.

Her father's poor health, coupled with his age, would not allow him to make the trip, and her brother's business needed their full attention. The letter ended with an invitation for Emmie to come to New York City for a reunion with them. There was no mention of Luke in the invitation, and this omission weighed heavily on Emmie's heart. Were her brothers and her father assuming his inclusion in the invitation, or were they deliberately omitting him? Could it be possible that they were biased against him because of his Indian blood? If this were so, then her long search for her family had been in vain, for she would never go to the city without him. She was his wife, and she wore her gold ring with great pride. It was true, of course, that the ceremony that had united them was not of the White Man's or Christian faith, but Emmie felt it just as binding, and made all this very clear in her return letter to her brother, Charles. She sent the letter by the first boat eastward, and walked with slow steps and a heavy heart back to the store.

She had not mentioned the letter to Luke, and this added to her depression. They had always shared their joys and problems and this was a new experience for her, but she was determined that this must be her secret, at least until she should receive a reply. And so, she put it all from her mind and resumed her spring cleaning chores with, if possible, more vigor than before. Luke was amused with the intensity with which she went about cleaning, not knowing, of course, the heavy secret she carried in her heart.

When both their living quarters and the store were spotless, she and Luke designed a new sign to be erected atop the new porch. When they had taken over the Post from Mrs. Becker, they hadcontinued on with the Becker name, but now the decision had been made to convert to a general store, and so they both felt that it was time to have a new sign. They wanted the name to be catchy, but plain, and so, since they were both well-known to the stage coach riders and canal men as Luke and Emmie, they settled on "The L&E General Store and Inn."

Luke worked for weeks to make the sign just right, and to secure it to the porch roof. He gathered white birch limbs and branches, and cut and shaped them to form the letters. These he mounted on some well-weathered planks that had been left over when they had built the Inn. The sign could readily be seen from the canal, and brought many flattering comments from the travelers.

The sign was up and the ground had been worked, and the gardens planted before an answer arrived to Emmie's letter. She was overjoyed at what she read. Of course Luke would be welcome in their home. And, as she read on, she realized that she should have had more faith in her family than to think they would exclude Luke from their reunion.

She tried to explain all this to Luke, and although he did not quite understand her explanation, he trusted her and agreed to go to New York City and meet with her long-lost family.

Emmie was so excited that for several days she did not accomplish much in the way of preparing for their journey. Luke sent her off to tell Maria her news, and seek Maria's help in fashioning a new wardrobe for the occasion. Emmie had some fine silk material that had arrived at Christmas time from Ellen, and she thought it would make a very appropriate dress for this coming special occasion.

George watched the women work throughout the warm spring evenings, and smiled to himself at how well they worked together. Had they been sisters, he thought, they would not have been closer.

Although Maria had never drawn or painted, she had a distinctive artistic ability, and her ideas, when transferred to the fine material, were most successful. With the dress finished, with material left over, they made a shirt for Luke. She had sent measurements and instructions to a tailor in Utica before leaving for the Swenson's, and a message of urgency, promising a bonus if he carried out her instructions. Neither had ever had anything except homemade clothing, and she felt certain that for this occasion, something special was in order.

The sewing finished, Emmie rode back home with her precious garments wrapped in a leather bag Luke had made for her during the winter. Ebony trotted along the now well-worn trail, and their ride seemed to take less timethan ever before. They stopped only long enough for a quick lunch and were home well before supper time.

Both Emmie and Luke were kept busy for the next several days, giving instructions and making sure that everyone knew what would be expected of them while they were away. The O'Donnells would run the Inn, and the O'Neilswould tend the store. The old hunchback, who had been with the Becker's, and had stayed on all these years with them, had passed away while Emmie had been at the Swenson's, and they had buried him near the big oak tree, where the Beckers had been buried. He had no relatives that anyone knew about. He had never spoken of any family, and, in fact, they had never known his family name. He had always been Zeb to them. A soft-spoken, hunchbacked man who had lived alone in a little shed to the south of the Post. He had worked for his keep and the few trinkets they had given him over the years. He would be sorely missed, for although they both realized that he must be very old, his strength had never lessened with age, and he had been a tremendous asset to them. After his burial, Emmie asked Luke to pack his meager possessions and bring them to her, and that evening she sat before the fireplace (for it was a cool spring evening), and sorted through them, thinking that she might find a clue as to who he was, and where he had come from. But no clue was found, and so, the next morning Luke buried the neatly packed crate beside him, and closed an era in their lives, the last link to the Beckers, and the old trading post.

CHAPTER VII

Emmie's heart was filled with mixed emotions. The valley was so beautiful in the spring--the ice floes in the river had passed, and the canal had been opened for travel. The flowers that seemed to spring from nowhere were everywhere in bloom. Jack-in-thepulpits, May-flowers and the deep, soft purple of the first violets. The mountains rose majestically to the north, dressed in their many shades of green, with the firs so dark and stately, and the maples, elms, birches and ash bursting into leaf; and scattered through this maze were the pink and white blossoms of the wild fruit trees. The smell of newness and freshness was everywhere, and it was the season that Emmie loved best of all the seasons. And yet, she knew she must leave all this and go to the great city and the reunion of her family. Luke, too, was having these same thoughts, but he didn't confide in Emmie, lest she decide against going to New York City, and he knew they must go if she were ever to see her father again.

CHAPTER VIII

They had arrived in Utica at noon and gone directly to the tailor whom Emmie had engaged to make Luke's waistcoat and britches, and when Luke had dressed in the new finery, Emmie could hardly believe her eyes. He stood so straight and tall; Emmie thought he surely would be the most handsome man she would ever see.

They ate lunch at Bagg's Tavern, and were ready to resume their journey when the next packet appeared from the west.

The afternoon passed rapidly with stops at all the places that they had both heard about from the travelers who stopped at their Inn and store.

The bell towers on the court houses in both Herkimer and Fonda could be seen rising above the other buildings, and the stone church at Fort Herkimer stood majestically alone on the south shore of the river. Neither went below to sleep, as the excitement they both felt prevented any thought of sleep from overcoming them, and as they sat together, wrapped in a blanket on the prow of the packet, they watched as the walls of the canal silently slipped past in the moonlight. Before anyone else stirred about the next morning, Emmie opened their hamper, and they breakfasted on cold meat and biscuits.

They disembarked at the Port in Albany, and boarded a much larger boat to take them down the Hudson River to their destination. On this boat they had a tiny room to themselves, and although it was hot an stuffy, and the bunks were hard, they were both ready for a rest and a LONG sleep. They removed only their outer garments, and Emmie noted that Luke hung, with great pride, his new coat on a peg behind the door. And, she thought, how much of the White Man's ways he practiced, and how many of his ancestor's habits had seemingly been forgotten, until, after a few moments of lying down on the hard straw mattress, he wished aloud for some fresh, soft hemlock boughs.

Emmie had always referred to the Mohawk River as "The Great River," but as they came on deck the first morning of their trip down the

Hudson River, she stood in utter amazement at the great expanse of water on either side of the boat. The distance to either shore was greater than the whole of her "Great River," and as they glided over the seemingly motionless water, she could see the Catskill Mountains rise on their right. They were as majestic, indeed, as the tales the travelers had told, though not as high as her beloved Adirondacks, but majestic, none the less.

Both were constantly amazed at the traffic on the river. Both large and small craft, in either direction.

The boats and ships were much larger and far more luxurious than any that passed the Post on the Erie Canal, and were powered, not by mules pulling them along the banks, but by great paddle wheels powered by steam engines. The ships had great stacks from which bellowed great rolls of smoke. There were the passenger ships like the one they were on, and then smaller tugs pulling strings of barges. There were also sail boats, canoes and small boats manned by men with oars and paddles. Both Emmie and Luke were ecstatic at the sights they passed. Besides the boats going up and down the river there were ships and ferries crossing from side to side as the expanse of the river was too great for bridges. They saw factories and plants and there were great kilns where bricks were being made, bringing back to Emmie memories of the dirt and clay bricks she and Luke had made for the fireplace in the little mountain cabin, where they had first lived after they were married. And they could see great cave openings in the mountains where men dug out cement for the bricks. The farms were large and picturesque, and there were great orchards ablaze with the pink and white blossoms of apples, pears and peaches. They could see large gangs of Negroes, watched over by white men on horses, working in the fields; and when they passed Poughkeepsie, the half-way mark, they observed great factories - tall buildings as yet strangers to their area.

The crews on the boats and ships all seemed to know each other, waving and shouting as they passed. They were surprised too, at the accommodations on the river boat. The packets were a means of transportation, faster and more comfortable than the horse and wagon, bumping over the well-rutted trails, but Emmie confided to Luke that these boats were, by those standards, luxurious indeed. A private compartment for sleeping - a dining room where meals were served, and chairs where one could sit on deck and enjoy the river breezes and the scenery. Most of the barges and cargo boats stopped often, but theirs was mainly a passenger vessel, and so stopped only for discharging or picking up passengers at the larger docks.

As they passed the Military Academy at West Point, the cadets could be seen parading and practicing their military maneuvers, and the passengers all gathered at the rail to watch until they were well past, and darkness was closing in on them, when the bell for the evening meal sounded.

Sleep did not come easily to either, that second night from the Port of Albany. Although they were both tired, they were overly excited about their arrival in New York City the next morning, and the anticipation of the long-awaited meeting with Emmie's family.

Emmie was so excited that all she managed to consume at breakfast was a cup of steaming coffee, which she carried on deck so that she would not miss a moment of their approach to the city. As their boat slipped up to the dock, and the gang plank was let out, Emmie and Luke were the first passengers to walk down to the waiting crowd. As Emmie peered over the many faces, her eyes searched for Chris, for she thought he was the only one she might recognize. When she spotted him at last, he was not alone, but a young girl was at his side, and both Emmie and Luke stopped in stark amazement, for seeing her was like seeing Emmie many years ago. Had Luke not had his arm around her, Emmie felt as though she might have stumbled and fallen. As she looked up at Luke his face was ashen--a second Princess! surely he was not yet awake.

Emmie's long blond hair was now streaked with silver, and she wore it braided and twirled around her head, giving her a majestic appearance. Her fair skin, although smooth and supple, was permanently bronzed from years of exposure to the wind and sun. The young girl beside Chris, a slim, beautiful blond, a perfect replica of the old Emmie, was waving and jumping up and down with anxiety and excitement, and when they finally met, threw her arms around Emmie, and then, in silence, they walked to a waiting carraige.

Chris took the bag containing their few belongings from Luke and tossed it to the driver, and as soon as they were all seated, directed him where to take them.

Emmie recognized the address as the one she had directed her letters when writing to her brother. Chris, remembering his manners, introduced the young girl that Emmie and Luke sat silently staring at as Mary, his sister, and Emmie recalled fleetingly, for the first time in years, that Ma's given name had been Mary.

Neither Emmie or Luke heard much of the conversation, and Emmie wondered later if they had answered intelligibly, for both were so excited. Neither had ever ridden in a carriage before. They had, of course, seen wagons and stage coaches pass the Post, but had never ridden in any conveyance, other than on horse back, until they had started on this trip on a canal packet. The girl, Emmie noticed, was finely dressed in silk, and wore a bonnet and gloves, and carried a small draw-string bag. But she had little time to ponder over this as their carriage soon drew up to a tall brownstone house, surrounded by a high iron fence.

As soon as the carriage stopped, Emmie wanted to jump out, but was restrained by Luke's hand on her arm, and they waited for the driver to alight and assist them, first to a large square of limestone, and then to a brick walkway. Chris and Mary led the way up the walk to the front door and rang a bell. Emmie's heart nearly stopped, for she thought they must be at some stranger's house if they had to ring before entering. Almost immediately a Negro, dressed in clothes that Emmie thought were finer than Luke's, answered and bade them enter, addressing Chris and Mary as Master and Mistress, and led them to a large room on the left of the hall, that was lined with books, and announced that Mr. Charles would be down directly.

Emmie sank into the nearest chair, and Luke stepped to her side. As she looked about her at the rows of books and the polished furniture, she knew in her heart that she had an awful lot to learn about the way these people, her family, lived.

They were there but a few minutes when Chris came in, escorting a very old man, whom Emmie could, in no stretch of her imagination, associate with the tall vibrant father she remembered from her youth. But when he spoke, the old verve was in his voice, a voice so authorative that both Emmie and Luke sprang to what an onlooker might interpret as military attention. The tone of authority that Emmie remembered so well as a child was still there. The tenderness with which he touched her hand, and the strong handshake with which he greeted Luke, were all mannerisms she had so long associated with the memories of her father, the memories that she had carried in her mind these many long years. But she had never really thought of him as an old man. All these years he had remained young in her mind. During the short silence that fell over the little group, Emmie's mind went back almost forty years to the day Ma and she stood on the south bank of the Mohawk River and waved to and watched Papa and the boys until they were out of sight down the river, on their way to the Port of Albany to trade their winter's accumulation of furs and skins for supplies, and perhaps a few small coins, if they fared well. So many things had occurred in Emmie's life since she had waved good-bye to him for a supposed two weeks separation that had lasted these many years. Surely those years had changed Papa, too. There were no visible remnants of that tall young man left in this old, stooped person that stood before her. Luke's hand on Emmie's shoulder brought her back to reality, and she began hearing the words that this stranger (her father) was directing to her.

Did she have a pleasant trip? And would she like to freshen up and rest a bit before dinner? Emmie seized this opportunity to leave the group that had assembled, and to be alone and collect her thoughts.

The room that she was directed to was on the second floor. A room, Emmie thought, to be nearly as large as her whole house. Her thoughts returned to the day she and Luke had moved to the Post with Mrs. Becker. It had surpassed all of Emmie's ideas of elegance, but in no way could it now compare with the grandeur that surrounded her here.

Disregarding the exhaustion that was rapidly consuming her, both mentally and physically, Emmie spent the first several minutes in the room absorbing and admiring the grandeur that was all around her. There were many things in the room that Emmie had never seen before, even in pictures in catalogs. Silver and crystal appointments on a dressing table, with all sorts of exciting aromas emitting from several small jars, each time Emmie lifted a cover. A tap on the door brought her back to reality. As Emmie opened the door she was greeted by two young girls in crisp, white uniforms, one carrying a great kettle of steaming water, and the other a stack of what Emmie found to be towels.

Emmie stepped aside as they entered, and watched in amazement as they bustled about the room. The girl with the water opened a door to a small ante-room and exposed a large, oval vat-like tub, which Emmie was soon to learn was a bath tub, into which she was expected to sit and bathe. The other girl had picked up Emmie's bag and was taking out the meager contents. Emmie had packed very little; a night dress, a calico skirt and waist, the new silk dress, a supple suede tunic and trousers and a pair of moccasins. Nearly the same for Luke; a night shirt Emmie wasn't sure she could get him to wear. She had made it especially for the trip, but Luke was not in favor of dressing for bed. An extra shirt and tunic, trousers and moccasins like the ones she had brought for herself; a few undergarments for herself completed their entire wardrobe. Beneath the moccasins she lifted out a very heavy pouch, which, before she could open it, Emmie took from her, and at this act, the girl showed the first signs of emotion. She had contained her surprise at the contents of the bag, as the pouch accounted for the extreme weight of the bag. She had never seen such a pouch before, and could not imagine why it was so secret. No guests in all her time with the Van der Veers had ever brought such a strange array of clothing. Emmie was also the only guest she had attended that brought only one bag for both husband and wife.

Emmie would have been happier if she had known that Luke was across the hall, going through the same experiences as she. At the same time the maid was wondering if she would be able to attend the needs of this lady who was so very different from any other guest she had ever attended. Emmie was standing, clutching the pouch, her arms aching from its weight as it contained their money; several hundred dollars in gold and silver

Before they had started on their trip to New York City, Luke had made a secret hiding place for their money, for they could not bring it all with them. Some had to be left for the O'Donnells and O'Neils to run the Inn and the store, since up until now all their business had been cash or trade transactions. Living as they did, on the edge of the wilderness, they had not been able to use the new public financial institutions called banks that they had heard and read about. They had, since the canal had opened, accepted some paper money from travelers and Emmie was more inclined than Luke to believe in this currency. Now she was wishing that she had brought paper instead of gold and silver, for the pouch was heavy, and as she glanced around the room, she saw no place where she thought it might be safe.

At this point, the girl who had been busying herself in the ante-room announced that Madam's bath was ready. Emmie was astounded. All her life she had cleansed her body by bathing in the creek in the warm weather, from a water basin in the winter time. She was not about to disrobe in front of two strangers, and step into this vat-like affair that had been filled with steaming water.

She quickly composed herself, and in a voice as steady as she could manage, dismissed both young women. They left, reluctantly.

When she was at last alone, she put the pouch back in the bag and placed it on the floor of the closet where her clothes had been hung. Emmie was amazed at the size of the clothes closet. Nearly the size of their whole bedroom at the Post, she thought. There were pegs all along two sides, and the third side was devoted to shelves. Surely, Emmie thought, no one person could have enough garments to fill a room like this.

She quickly undressed and hung her traveling clothes next to her tunic and felt relieved indeed to be free from the close-fitting garments. She cautiously stepped back into the main room and dashed across to the ante-room, where the tub of hot water was waiting. The aroma of fresh flowers filled the room, and Emmie found, as she glanced around, that the odor was coming from the water, and she could not understand how that could possibly be. She also saw that that there was no other place provided to wash away the dirt and grime of travel, and so, with great reluctance, she put one foot in the tub.

The water was very warm, and seemed soft and soothing, and so she finally found herself sitting in this strange contraption, and splashing water all around.

There were cloths and bars of fragrant, colored soap on a nearby stand, and Emmie chose a pink bar that smelled to her like wild roses. She scrubbed her body until she thought to herself that her skin was as pink, and smelled like the soap itself.

As she finished her bathing and stepped out of the tub, she chose another, much larger cloth, and rubbed her body dry, and quickly dressed in her calico skirt and blouse, and after much contemplation, put on the shoes and stockings she had traveled in. She left her long hair hanging loose about her shoulders.

Cautiously, she opened the door to the hall, and was greeted by the two young girls she had dismissed. No words were passed between them, and as they stepped aside, Emmie found her way to the stairway, and quickly descended to the floor below, from which rose the voices of those she had left there. When she entered the room, she found that they had been joined by several others, and Charles quickly rose, and started to introduce Emmie to the newcomers: his wife, Anna, his second daughter, Charlotte, and Lum, Emmie's younger brother, stood to their right.

She always remembered Lum as so very tall and strong; muscles bulging from beneath his shirt. She remembered the day Luke had found her, bathing in the creek, and how he had reminded her of Lum. Many years had passed since that day, and although Lum was still tall, he no longer seemed to Emmie to be the lean, strong man she had remembered all this time. His hair was very white, and his shoulders, as he stood to greet Emmie, were stooped with age. A man,

Emmie thought, more like she might have remembered her father than her brother. But when he hugged her, and spoke in her ear, she knew it to be Lum. He had always secretly called her "Em," and with that name ringing in her ear, the reunion turned into a tearful, yet joyful, affair. He took Emmie's hand from Charles, and they walked together around the room, Lum speaking ever so softly, and introducing her to each one there.

There were the sisters-in-law, and the children, and the husbands and wives of children, fifteen in all, and by the time the introductions had been completed, Emmie's head was spinning, and she wondered if she would ever be able to get all these people straightened out in her mind. She didn't have but a moment to mull this over before Luke entered, his eyes bright with excitement and wonder at all he had seen on the upper floor. He was, of course, still dressed in his traveling clothes, because his possessions had been in the single bag that had been placed in the room assigned to Emmie. The thought quickly passed through her mind that she would have to speak to Lum about some different arrangements. She and Luke must be allowed to share the same quarters. She realized at that moment that Luke was the only person in this gathering that she really knew, and they would have to be together.

Emmie asked Lum to introduce Luke as he had for her, for as yet, everyone's name was but a confused jumble of words to her. After Luke had made the circle and had met everyone, he came and stood by Emmie's chair, and whispered softly that they must chat alone. His was even a worse predicament than hers, as she had the luggage, and he had had to put back on his traveling clothes, and he did not trust these large vats of water and sweet-smelling soaps. If their visit was to be more than a day or two, some other arrangements for clothing would have to be made, as the supply they had brought would not only be exhausted, but very inappropriate for the society with which they found themselves surrounded.

CHAPTER IX

Dinner was announced, and Emmie's father stood up and took her arm, and they headed the procession down the hall and into the dining room, a room that even in her wildest dreams Emmie would never have been able to imagine.

A long table covered with an ornate linen cloth, fine china, trimmed with gold bands, crystal goblets and several pieces of silverware on either side of the large plates, and across each plate a smaller folded cloth that matched the one covering the table. Candleabras at either end, filled with lighted candles, and a chandelier hanging from the ceiling, also filled with lighted candles, filled the room with light.

Emmie was seated next to her

father, who sat at the head of the table. Charles' wife, Anna, sat at the foot, and the rest seemed to know the places designated for them. Only Luke stood aside, and when everyone else was seated, he took the remaining empty seat, near the center on the left side.

Great heaping plates of food were passed about, and everyone seemed quiet and apparently interested in their food. Wine was poured into the goblets and Emmie glanced up the side of the table, seeking out the place where Luke sat, and as she did, she noticed that no one was really eating, but watching to see what Luke was doing.

"Why," Emmie thought, "they think of Indians as savages." Then she recognized the startled expressions on their faces as he picked up his utensils and proceeded to eat (as normally as anyone else). The silence was appalling. What did these people, her family, expect from one who was now their brother?

There was little conversation as the dinner proceeded. Everyone now seemed still engrossed in their own food. It seemed to Emmie that there was an endless number of people taking away and bringing new dishes to the table. There was one young man whose sole duty appeared to be to keep everyone's wine glass filled. Emmie noted that Luke had not touched his glass of wine, and so she did not either.

Emmie's thoughts returned to many years ago, when she was recovering at the Indian compound, before she was married to Luke, the old chief had been very much against"firewater," as he termed the White Man's brew, and had preached about it to Luke and the other braves. So she and Luke had never had any such beverages in their home or at the trading post. Emmie knew there was a great difference in the potency between wine and rum, but had never discussed this with Luke.

She remembered Ma making some sort of wine drink from wild elderberries and honey, and that Papa often drank from this jug when it was very cold, but never more than a small glassful. As Emmie sat quietly, her thoughts years away, more dishes were brought in and taken away, and finally a plate with a small bowl of warm water and another linen napkin was placed before her. She had never heard or seen anything like this before in her life. As these bowls were placed before each one, they seemed to stick their fingers in them, and then dabble with their napkins to dry their fingers, and then the bowls were whisked away.

Emmie followed the others, and so did Luke. He grinned at Emmie, as if to say, "How strange. What is it with these people?" but of course, not aloud. After the bowls were gone her father rose, and the men followed him to the library, where Emmie and Luke had been greeted earlier in the day. The room where Emmie had seen more books than she had ever imagined existed.

Anna rose, and the women followed her to the opposite side of the hall, into a room that Emmie was to later learn, was called the drawing room. The name mystified Emmie. Drawing had always meant pictures on slate or paper, or even in the sand with a stick. Emmie was soon to learn new meanings for familiar words. It was true there were drawings on the wall; great paintings and portraits, but she was sure no one ever drew pictures in this room. And as she studied the paintings hung on the walls, she felt a sense of recognition as her eyes rested upon one of the high mountains so familiar to her.

As soon as the ladies were all seated, a servant came in with a tray with tiny cups and an elegant coffee pot, and served them all with a cup of very black, very hot, very bitter beverage. It tasted to Emmie like burned coffee, and as she sipped at hers, she wondered if Luke was being served the same beverage, and if so, what his reaction was.

Emmie need not have fretted about Luke. He was enjoying himself immensely. He had refused a cigar when the box was passed to him, and had, instead, taken out his old clay pipe, and lighted it, to the amusement of everyone, with a kindling from the wood box beside the hearth. He sensed their amusement and decided to play along with their idea that he was a savage. As he silently puffed away, he toyed with the idea of passing his pipe to Lum, who was standing by the mantle to his right. But while he was toying with this thought, another servant entered the room with a tray holding a large crystal decanter and glasses. Should he accept, and not drink? Should he drink and do a few steps of a war dance? He was sure this was what they expected.

"Oh dear, where is Emmie?" he thought. These were her people, and he wanted her to as proud of him as he had been of her when he had taken her to his people those many years ago.

The decision came quickly to him: he would go to his room, saying he was tired from the trip. He wasn't tired, and he had never before in his life told an untruth, but he felt that this was what he must do now. Everyone in the room made a lot of small talk, and Chris walked to the bottom of the stairway with him and patted his arm knowingly. He went to the room where he had earlier rested before the evening meal.

Emmie was listening without really hearing what the women were discussing. Social events, clothing--things that to Emmie were not part of Luke and her lives. She looked around the room and suddenly felt very alone. More alone than she had felt since the fire, and had been lost in the mountains. She had never in all those long years realized how much she depended on Luke. She longed for Luke to scoop her up in his arms and carry her away from all this grandeur that was so foreign to her; to take her back to the little store and Inn; to the little schoolroom where she taught the O'Donnell and O'Neil and Violet's children the fundamentals of life: letters and numbers and how to read and write.

She was suddenly aware that Anna was addressing her, asking if she would like to go to the art museum and see a display of paintings by a newly discovered artist. A young girl who had been discovered by a wealthy traveling salesman, whom she had married and who had brought her from poverty in the mountains to the city, where her works had been acclaimed as exceptional. A style all her own, of paintings of animals and Indians and nature in its wildest form. She had, Anna continued, painted the picture that Emmie had felt to be so familiar - Ellen's work!

Emmie had never considered the Swenson's or herself as poor. In fact, they were among the wealthiest people, with the exception of a few travelers, that Emmie had ever known until now. Wealth was not measured in the Upper Mohawk Valley and Adirondack Mountains as it was seemingly measured in this great city.

Emmie wondered how Ellen had acclimated to this new life. Her letters had sounded so happy, and her life so full. She was anxious to see her and how she lived; and she was sure she could learn a great deal about these city dwellers from her. She had written to her about their trip, and was sure that if Ellen knew these people, she would get in touch with them very soon. But to go and view the exhibit without her didn't seem right to Emmie, and to Anna's astonishment, Emmie related her relationship with Ellen. And not meaning to brag or be rude in any way, told Anna of the many pictures that they had in their home that Ellen had done. Anna was completely surprised at this revelation, but assured Emmie that it was a public gallery, and that Ellen would probably be there.

Besides being great admirers of Ellen's work, the Van der Veers and Wilsons were social friends. The Van der Veer men had been business associates when Mr. Wilson was a salesman, and when he had married and brought his wife to the city and had opened the art gallery, the women had met and had become socially friendly. What Anna did not understand was that if Emmie knew this artist so well, why surely Ellen would have mentioned to them that she knew a Van der Veer family as a young girl in the Mohawk Valley.

Emmie was going on with her tale about Ellen's mother being her best friend, and that Ellen had lived with she and Luke before being married, and, in fact, had been married at the Inn, and how anxious she was to see Ellen now. What neither of the women knew was how Mr. Wilson felt about Indians; how prejudiced he was against the Red Skins, and Luke was no exception.

And so, without further consultation, it was decided that this is what they would do tomorrow. Almost as soon as the decision was made, the men joined them. No one mentioned the absence of Luke, and so Emmie spoke quietly to Chris about his whereabouts. Upon hearing that he had retired to his room across the hall from hers, Emmie immediately said good night to everyone and left the room. She found Luke at the window of his room, gazing out over the expanse of buildings, with their lighted windows, and to the harbor beyond. Even through the darkness one could sense the activity and enormity of the city. Emmie had, over the years, learned many of the Indian's ways, but one of their traits, that of silence in walking and stillness had evaded her. Even though she had been quiet, she was not quiet enough for Luke's keen ears, and as he turned, Emmie ran to him, and threw her arms about him and clung to him for ever so long.

They walked in silence across the wide hall to the room assigned to her, and began preparing for bed. Luke was amused at the new fancy nightshirt Emmie had made for him, and pranced around the room, hopping first on one foot and then the other. He grasped Emmie in his arms and swung her around until the whole room seemed to be spinning like a toy top, and they fell, laughing, to the floor.

A light tapping at the door brought them to a standstill, and as Emmie bade the rapper to come in, Luke quickly slid beneath the coverlet. A very startled maid entered, wanting to know if Emmie would like some assistance in preparing for the night. Emmie was now standing in the middle of the spinning room in her undergarments, and felt that she must have presented a strange sight to the servant, for the look on her face was of complete surprise.

Emmie refused her help with a "No, thank you," and could hardly contain the laughter she felt welling up in her throat at the look of consternation on the young girl's face, when she spied the great heap that was Luke under the coverlet. He, of course, should be in the room across the hall. So, to relieve the girl's anxiety, Emmie announced that Mr. Van der Veer would be spending the rest of their visit in this room, with her, and it was the look on the girl's face that suddenly brought the realization to Emmie that Luke was not really being accepted as her husband, even by the servants.

Anger welled up in her heart, and she had a great desire to go downstairs and tell them all how she felt about Luke; how he had saved her after the fire, and had forsaken his people to marry her, and had left his native ways and his own people to go and live a foreign life with her. But good sense quickly came to her, and she dismissed the girl and quickly got into bed beside Luke. Her whole body was shaking, but with Luke's strong arms around her, she quickly calmed down, and exhausted from the day's activities. she fell into a deep sleep.

Luke was already up and dressed when Emmie awoke. He had awakened early from many years of habit, but had not ventured out of the room. He had pondered, since waking, whether or not to discuss with Emmie his feelings about her family. He felt that Chris was the only one who really accepted him.

The rest, he was sure, expected him to do something savage and wild, but he was not quite sure what. He had lived the White Man's ways for a long time and had always felt that their habits were, in many ways, crueler than the Indians' and he was at a complete loss as to what action to take. His keen ears had noted that they had not introduced him as Emmie's husband; only as "Luke." He liked being Emmie's Mr. Van der Veer, even though they were seldom addressed that way. Almost everyone who came to the old trading post had known them as Emmie and Luke. But his Princess had given him her name, and he meant to keep it. It was on the deed to their lands in the mountains, and the papers that Mrs. Becker had sent them when the trading post had become officially theirs.

He knew all eyes had been on him in the dining room, and in the library when he lit his pipe. He really wanted to leave this great city, and hurry back to the safety of their life in the Valley of the Great Mohawk, and in the shadow of "his" beloved Adirondacks.

When her heard Emmie stir, he sat down on the side of the bed beside her, and took her in his arms. He quickly and quietly told her of his feelings, and suggested that they return to their home as quickly as possible. She agreed with him, but felt she must see Ellen before they left, and told him of the plans to visit the gallery where her art was on exhibit. She quickly dressed and they both then joined those already in the dining room for breakfast. Neither had much of an appetite, but felt they must at least pretend to participate in the meal.

Emmie's father, at the head of the table, made it known that he felt everyone should eat a hearty breakfast. After Emmie and Luke were excused, and about to leave the room, Anna spoke of their planned visit to the art gallery,and suggested that Emmie would no doubt like to change her clothes for something more suitable for the trip downtown.

Emmie's wardrobe was very limited, and although courtesy kept her from any unpleasant reply, she simply nodded and quickly left the room.

She went first to Luke's room and then to hers, and quickly packed their meager belongings. She dressed, as did Luke, in their traveling clothes, and they went together to find Emmie's father and explain their plans to him. They would go to the gallery, and if Ellen was not there, they would call at her home, and from there would go to the river docks and take the night liner back up the river.

They found the elder Mr. Van der Veer in the library, and without preamble, told him their plans. He roared his objections and became excited to the point that both Emmie and Luke were afraid for his health, but his weakened state seemed to grow immediately stronger as he turned his wrath on Luke, saying things that Emmie felt unforgivable. But as she started to retort, Luke put his strong hand on her arm in a restraining gesture, and he replied to Mr. Van der Veer in a soft and pleasant tone.

He quietly explained what he and Emmie had discussed earlier. Emmie was so proud of him! His command of the English language was far beyond many well educated white men, although the ugly word "savage," had reared up in her father's diatribe, there was not a trace of savagery in his manner. Nor could Emmie ever remember any such trait in him, or any of the tribe she had known. She recalled his soft-tempered mannered old father. The "Chief," who had relinquished his hold over Luke, and bade him go with Emmie and take up the ways of the White Man.

She felt both shame and sorrow forher father. He was condemning Luke without any true knowledge of him or his people. The old man was trembling with rage, and as he continued to say unforgivable things about Luke, he also included Emmie, saying things that as they fell on her ears, Emmie knew in her heart that he could not really believe. She felt no remorse toward her father when the ranting stopped; only sorrow that the loving, kind father that she had remembered all these years; the man that she prayed to find, should so condemn not only her savior and husband, but she as well.

She took Luke's hand, and they left the room in silence. They shared each other's feelings - feelings that came from being so close so many years. They had never solved their problems with loud and angry words, and now was not the time to start.

As they closed the library door behind them, leaving Mr. Van der Veer to ponder the distance he had put between them, they met a maid who informed Emmie that Anna was ready to go to the art museum. Emmie waited in the great hall, while Luke returned to their room for their traveling bag. Anna appeared at the same time Luke came downstairs with the bag, and a questioning look came over her face as she came upon them in their traveling clothes, with bag in hand.

Emmie, feeling that an explanation was needed, explained that she and Luke would be taking the river liner to Albany, and would go directly to the pier from the gallery. Anna was momentarily silenced by Emmie's statement. She had not overheard any of the angry words that had been spoken in the library, nor had she guessed at the unhappy state of Emmie and Luke.

She had been born and brought up in the city, and even though she had been both shocked and amused by knowledge of her husband Charles' revelation that he even had a sister, she was pleased when they had arrived, and personally was very taken with the handsome Luke. To her knowledge, there had been no Indians in the city for many years, and she was quite fascinated with having one as a guest in her home.

One could hardly find any expressly Indian traits in Luke, for he was dressed and acted as a white man. In fact, she thought, he was a much more gracious man than many of Charles' business associates who often called at their home, and his gentleness toward Emmie was very touching. She regained her composure and questioned them as to the change in their plans. The ensuing silence seemed endless until Luke replied that they were needed at their business in the valley.

The ride to the gallery was silent. Emmie's thoughts were very confused. A lifetime of searching - hoping to be found by her family, only to have her father reject Luke. How could he not see the wonderful qualities in him that were so evident to her? No one who had ever stopped at the Post had ever shown the slightest fear or rejection of him in any way, and the Swensons had been like brother and sister to them; accepting Luke without question, and Mrs. Becker, who had every right to question Indians, having lost her first husband in a bloody battle with Indian warriors (led by Tories), and had accepted him as a son.

Her father, she felt, had no reason for his feelings. He had had, in his early life, more conflicts with his Tory neighbors than with the Indians. And after all, it was the Tories who had enticed the Indians over to their side with promises of great wealth and power.

There were several people at the gallery when they arrived, and they had been there some time before they spotted Ellen talking with some patrons, viewing a portrait of an Indian, which bore a remarkable resemblance to Luke.

She seldom did portraits, and the Indian warrior had been a bone of contention between she and her husband. He had made it very clear that he held no love in his heart for Red Skins and that he did not want the painting hung in the gallery. But Ellen had insisted. She never crossed or contradicted Mr. Wilson, for she had learned early in their marriage that he had a very spicy temper, and her life was much more pleasant if she did his bidding. But she felt this painting must be hung, and she had argued until he had agreed.

She had not mentioned Emmie and Luke to the Van der Veers, or had she written to Emmie about her new friends by the same name as she and Luke went by. She felt very badly about this, but she also felt that any mention of them would cause much questioning on the part of the Van der Veers and that Mr. Wilson would be very upset with her.

When Ellen saw them, she excused herself and rushed to Emmie, embracing her in a long hug, but when Luke went to take her in his arms, she visibly stiffened and offered him her hand.

She felt most ashamed at her own actions, but knew they were being watched by Mr. Wilson, and she did not want any public confrontation. She already realized that Mr. Wilson had been civil to Luke in order to get to know her, and she wasn't sure what he might say. It was indeed coincidental that Emmie and Luke should arrive the very day that the painting of the Indian warrior was hung.

The awkward moment passed quickly, and they all chatted amiably. Luke realized immediately from the look on Ellen's face that her reactions were governed not by her, but by someone else.

Ellen was anxious for news of her father and mother and Jon and her Valley friends. The time passed quickly, and when they were departing, Ellen seemed disappointed that their visit was to end so abruptly, and that Emmie would not be able to see her home and studio.

They stopped at an Inn near the docks for an early supper, and Luke asked the Innkeeper to pack them a box of food for their trip, even though there would be meals served on the boat, he wanted something to take with them. When they reached the river docks they found that there would not be a boat up to Albany for some time. They both suggested that Anna should not wait, as it would no doubt be dark before they embarked.

She reluctantly agreed. She was sorry that their visit was coming to such an abrupt end, and felt that their business in the Valley had really no bearing on their sudden decision to leave. She wished desperately that Charles had been home that morning when they had left for the gallery. Certainly he would have had some influence on them, and would have demanded a more reasonable explanation for their leaving.

After a short but tearful farewell, Anna was about to order the driver on when two carriages drew up beside her with Charles, Christopher and Father Van der Veer in the first one, and Bertha and Lum in the other. Mr. Van der Veer broke the awkward silence by taking Luke's hand in his, and in a voice trembling with emotion, offered his apology for his earlier outburst that morning in the library.

"I'm a foolish old man who lost his only daughter once, and I don't want that to happen again," he said.

"Sometimes we don't see straight. We forget our heritage, and that this land that has given us so much was taken from your people," he continued.

Luke put Mr. Van der Veer's hand in both of his and held tight.

"No," he said. "My people fought with the British and lost, but my father, a wise old sage, saw far beyond his years to the progress that the new settlers were bringing to his country. He loved your daughter as a daughter of his own, and bade me give up my heritage and accept her ways.

She taught me the language I speak today, and by sharing our heritages we have a wonderful life together."

With tears in his eyes, Mr. Van der Veer turned and directed Charles to fetch the bag he had brought with him in the carriage.

"If they'll have me, I'm going home with my daughter and her husband," he announced. "Now, no talk about my poor health. My lungs are aching for some of that fresh valley and mountain air," he continued. "I want to feel the first frost of fall nip at my nose and tingle my toes. I want to hear the first robin singing in the pines in the spring, and I want to sit and watch the boats silently glide by on that wonderful new canal that crosses this great state we live in."

Before he had finished, Emmie

had her arms around him, but all she could say was "Dear Papa, dear Papa."

He directed his next words to Charles and Lum.

"I'll get some legal papers drawn up in Albany to make all we've built here in the city yours. I'll send a letter along with details of what I want from the house, and you can ship it to me. I'm going home," he exclaimed. "I'm going to get to know this new son of mine."

The good-byes that followed were tearful indeed. Tears of joy at the acceptance of Luke as one of them, and tears of sadness as they waved good bye to their newly-found family members.

CHAPTER X

Emmie was much too excited to sleep. They had gone to their cabin almost immediately upon leaving the dock and had lain down on the bunk. Emmie had slipped off only her dress and tried to lay quietly so as not to disturb Luke, and after she had listened for some time to his soft and even breathing, she slipped into her soft leather tunic and moccasins and went up on deck.

The river was quiet. The splashing of the wheel paddles the only sound to be heard. The banks seemed far away and the few lights twinkled like low stars on the horizon. It was here, alone on deck, that Luke found her when he had awakened and found her bunk empty. He became frightened. So many things had happened so quickly, he was afraid he had been dreaming and suddenly the tiny stateroom had seemed small and cramped, and so he slipped into his britches and rushed outside, not even bothering to put on moccasins, but with a terrific urge in his heart to find his Princess. They sat in silence, arms around each other, a long, long time, not talking or discussing the events of the evening, just sitting and holding each other.

The sky began to lighten, and some activity could be seen along the shore, and Luke went quickly and brought back the box of food that he had had packed at the tavern, and they ate ravishingly of the few goodies. When activity could be heard below deck, and the bell rang for breakfast, they went back to their room and freshened up. Luke put on his soft leather tunic and moccasins, and Emmie combed and braided her hair, but let the braid hang down her back. They emerged just in time to meet Papa and go for breakfast. Emmie and Luke, of course, were not hungry, having devoured to the last crumb of the food they had brought with them, but the steaming cups of coffee that were served tasted good and each drank several.

Emmie remembered Papa's words from the morning before, about a hearty breakfast, and tried to eat a little, but he was busy relishing the great plate of food that had been set before him, and did not seem to notice their lack of appetite. He was amazed at the conviences on board the river boat, and the ease with which the paddles seemed to propel them along. His trip down the river many years ago had been in a sail boat, and they had spread blankets and slept on deck. They had not been able to salvage anything from the fire, and as a result, had very little luggage, only the clothes that they wore.

When they had arrived home from their spring trip to the Port of Albany those many years before, they had been greeted, not by Emmie and Ma, but by complete desolation. All of their barns, outbuildings and even the animals were laying in a blackened ruin. The fire had burned everything to the ground, and the ashes had smoldered until nothing recognizable was left. They had searched frantically for some sign or clue as to what had happened to their loved ones. They had spread their search to the fields beyond and to the river banks without an answer.

After several days of searching and sifting through the scant remains, they decided to return down the river. They had stopped at each farm and settlement, inquiring about what might have happened to their little family and farm that had so mysteriously been completely destroyed by fire, but found no answer along the way.

They found themselves, several days later, back at the Port of Albany, but without answers to any of their questions. Their lives had been turned upside down, and all Papa and Ma had worked so hard for had all been lost. The decision was made to go to New York City and start anew. They would learn new trades and build new lives for themselves , and still be able to inquire of travelers for any clues or news of Emmie and Ma. The seeds and supplies that they had realized from their fur trading had been sold to neighbors, and the few coins from the sale of the supplies had jingled loosely in their pockets and helped pay their passage on the boat that was to take them to the great city and a new life.

Their struggle to make a living in the city had been very difficult. They had worked long, hard, tedious hours at jobs none of them were accustomed to. They had labored at the docks, loading and unloading heavy cargo, and for wages that were pitifully meager. They had lived in a rooming house that was cold in the winter and hot to the point of unbearability in the summer. Through all this they had saved until the two boys, with Papa's help, had been able to invest in the book company. Even after they had become a part of the company they had continued to labor long hours and had reinvested all money but what was needed for their personal needs until together they had been able to take over the company. While dock workers, they had inquired of all travelers from upstate about the whereabouts of any survivors from the fire. Although Papa helped the boys financially with their business, he never worked in the book company, but had continued to work on the docks until he began operating a small export business, never working in the book company. He knew furs from his early life in the Valley, and had, after his sons left the docks, invested and traded until he no longer had to work the docks but could spend all of his time trading and exporting. In doing this he felt that he had a closer tie to travelers and held out hope for many years of hearing of some news of what had happened to his wife and daughter.

They had all prospered and had together built the mansion where they now lived. The boys had married, and Papa had sold his business and retired. From the sale of his business, and from the interest he had in his sons' company, he had a very substantial income after retiring, and had now resigned himself to never knowing if Emmie and his wife had lived or died until Chris had come back in the fall with the news that he had found Emmie.

Emmie pointed out to Papa the many sights they had seen on their trip downstream, and exclaimed over many of the sights that they had missed. Papa and the boys had never, in these many years, returned to the Valley, and he was speechless at the many changes that had taken place.

When they arrived in the Port of Albany they took rooms at the tavern on Pearl Street so Papa could take care of the legal matters he had promised Lum and Charles that he would do.

It took several days to accomplish this, and while he was busy with his business, Emmie and

Luke had a wonderful time looking through the shops and stores and just generally taking in the sights. They found shops that specialized in just one commodity, and then shops that were more like their own little post, where one could find a great variety of wares.

Papa's business was finally concluded satisfactorily and they boarded a packet for home.

When they passed the place, late the following afternoon, where his little farm had been, Papa turned and clasped Emmie to him and held her tight for a long time.

Emmie and he had sat alone on for hours the night before, and Emmie had told him all about the fire. How there had been no time to save Ma or anything from the house. How she had run to the little cave by the river to escape the stampeding animals, and how, when she had made her very first trip to the valley, those many years ago, to trade Luke's furs, she had been satisfied by travelers that the fire had been started in the forest by lightning, and had spread quickly to their little farm, and that nothing had survived--including Ma.

The children playing in the yard of the store spotted them when they got off the packet and greeted them with welcoming shouts. Emmie pointed out to Papa the new sign, and as she looked at Luke, they both knew they were happy to be back.

Papa made the decision to stay at the Inn, feeling that he would be less imposing upon Luke and Emmie, but wouldstill be close by. He wanted to gradually get reacquainted with his daughter and to get to know this new son.

The first few days after their arrival, there seemed to be little time for just chatting. Luke and the O'Donnell and the O'Neil men were busy clearing land and making it ready for the new building, which was to be Emmie's school. The women folk were busy at the Inn, for the traffic westward was at its peak, and even overland travelers were numerous. The children, when not weeding the gardens and helping with everyday chores, were swimming in the canal.

Papa, as everyone now called the elder Mr. Van der Veer, busied himself with just becoming acquainted with everyone, and the little community that was rapidly developing around the old store. Joseph and

Little Luke, who was now nearly as tall as Joseph, came down the mountain for seeds and supplies, bringing with them Joseph's winter bounty of furs. Emmie was glad for news of Violet and the children's safe journey home from school.

Emmie had sent one of the O'Neil children to the Swenson's to let Maria and George know that she and Luke were home from the city, and that Papa Van der Veer had come to live with them. It was but a few days before they came to meet Emmie's father.

Instead of eating in the public dining room at the Inn, Emmie arranged to have the food brought to the house, and Luke had a make-shift table set up on the porch, and they all had a real party. Although he had made no mention of it, Emmie remembered that it was Papa's 90th birthday, and had a special surprise cake to culminate the meal. Papa was pleased with all the fuss and frivolity that centered around him.

Several days later, when Papa returned from exploring close by, he questioned Emmie about the three crosses under the great oak tree on the hill, and that evening, as they sat on the porch, Emmie told him the tale of the Beckers and the old hunchback who were buried there, and Papa expressed his desire to be, when his time came, laid to rest there also.

The summer quickly passed and before long the garden had to be harvested and stores laid in for the long winter ahead.

Joseph and Teka arrived late one afternoon, ready, after their summer's fun and chores, to start their studies. Joseph was especially anxious for more book learning, as he had already decided that he did not want to stay on the little mountain farm, but to travel to the great city that Papa Van der Veer had told him about. Teka was still quite shy with strangers, but was also anxious to learn more of the ways of the other children.

The little building that was to be their school was completed and classes started. Papa visited the school regularly, and could see first-hand the tremendous task Emmie had undertaken. And so, one evening, after they had concluded their meal, he approached Emmie with the idea of asking Charles' daughter, Charlotte, to join them and aid Emmie in her teaching duties. She was familiar with teaching methods, having attended schools in the city and in Virginia. Emmie was delighted, and so a letter was dispatched to Charles. The answer came in the form of Charlotte herself. It was decided that she would stay with Emmie and Luke in their spare room, but when the trunks that arrived on a later packet were brought to the house, the little room overflowed, and after inspecting their contents, it was decided to repack most of the city clothing and store them at the Inn, as there would be no need for the gowns and fancy dresses that they contained. Charlotte observed the classes for a few days and then Emmie had her take over the more advanced students, leaving only the youngest O'Donnells and O'Neils to Emmie.

Charlotte took to life in the

country and enjoyed her students as much as they enjoyed her, and it was with great reluctance that school was dismissed the following spring. Charlotte had her trunks packed and readied herself to return to the city with a solemn promise to return in the fall.

Life continued as before at the little settlement. Joseph came for his spring supplies and asked if Little Luke could stay on and work there as he was no longer interested in the little farm. Teka went reluctantly back with her father, but they all knew that it would not be long before she no longer wanted to return to the farm either.

CHAPTER XI

The canal traffic was exceptionally heavy that spring, and the new store was like, Emmie thought, a beehive with everyone bustling around. New stock that had been ordered last fall began arriving, and every day meant crates and boxes and barrels must be unloaded or stored. Papa seemed to thrive on all the excitement, but Emmie and Luke both fretted that he would try to do too much. He was not used to heavy work, and although he would retire early each evening, seemingly exhausted, he would be ready to again help the next morning.

When Chris arrived in early June on a selling trip west, the store was in a turmoil. Stock ordered, still arriving daily, and Emmie and Luke were at their wits end with what to do with all the extra merchandise they had ordered. Papa had gone over the river to meet the packet that Chris was expected to be on, and no one could have been more surprised than Chris at the smiling, robust man in work clothes that greeted him. This person could not possibly be his grandfather. Why, his grandfather was a very old man, who mostly grumbled at everyone at home, and who everyone, even his father, was a little in awe of. Who had been, everyone said, in delicate health for as long as Chris could remember.

Charlotte had returned home in the spring with tales about the change in Grandfather. But even her tales about him hadn't led Chris to expect the man that was now greeting him. They walked over the bridge and the short way to the Inn and store in silence, but when he saw the dilemma that Luke and Emmie were in, he forgot that his grandfather was an old man, and they both started carrying crates and boxes to the store room.

After the evening meal, when Luke and Papa were having their pipes on the porch, Chris questioned Emmie about the change in his grandfather--the man that everyone, including the O'Donnell and O'Neil children, called Papa.

Emmie explained as best she could about Papa working so hard. He seems so happy, and wants to be included in all the activities, she explained. Although he had his own quarters at the Inn and he was always ready, bright and early to do all he could.

Maria and George Swenson had been down for a visit, and had pleaded with Papa to ride home with them for a few days, but he would have none of it, not wanting to miss any of the activities at the Inn and store. The canal was always a source of great delight for him. Many times he had seen people traveling west that he had known in the city. Some had stopped to visit, and others had only shouted and waved as their packets passed. And of course he had known many of the traveling salespeople from his past business connections. He was at last a contented and happy man.

Chris decided this news couldn't wait, and could best be related to his parents in person. So, after a few nights at the Inn, he changed his plans and returned to New York City.

Without time to even let Emmie and Luke know their plans, the Van der Veers arrived in the Mohawk Valley. After Chris' exciting tales of Papa Van der Veer, they had decided they must see for themselves, and Charlotte was anxious to return permanently to the Valley. She had spent many hours since her return home in the spring, seeking out supplies for the little school, and had announced her plans to return and live with Emmie and Luke.

Their packet arrived in late afternoon, and as they walked toward the little compound, they spied Papa walking toward them, surrounded by the O'Donnell and O'Neil children, all with fishing poles.

Chris had been right. No one could rightly describe the change in him. He certainly didn't look like a tired and weary 90-year old man. They greeted him with hugs and handshakes, and he bade the children to go along fishing without him, and instead, accompanied the family back to the store. There, Emmie was just winding up the day's business. Upon hearing all the excited chatter, the O'Donnell and O'Neil women came running over from the Inn. There were introductions all around, and the O'Donnell and O'Neil women returned to the Inn to prepare extra food and rooms for all the unexpected guests.

Emmie's little house was crowded indeed, and with everyone talking at once, no one was making very much sense. So Luke invited the men out to the front porch so the ladies could get freshened up and calmed down. Lum and Charles could not believe the change in Papa. They had been prepared by Chris for a change, but neither could believe this person, rocking so calmly and enjoying his pipe, could possibly be the same cantankerous person they had lived with for so many years.

The children passed with a great string of river bass, and waved to them on their way home, but returned almost immediately to announce that dinner was ready for everyone at the Inn.

At breakfast the next morning, Papa had to be assured by

Lum and Charles that they had left the business in New York City in capable hands, and that they were completely satisfied that all was running smoothly while they were away. The women were fascinated with life in the Valley, and did not seem to miss any of the luxuries of their city homes.

Charles spoke to Luke about securing a piece of land adjacent to he and Emmie's Inn for a summer place for them.

Chris continued on west as he had originally been scheduled to do, and after a week of constant chatting they were ready to return to the city. Charlotte stayed, pleading that she had much to do to prepare for the fall classes, and Luke promised to look into purchasing the desired acreage for a summer place for Emmie's family.

After they had boarded the eastbound packet, and they had watched it well out of sight, Emmie, Luke and Papa strolled leisurely back to the Inn.

Luke and Papa set out for Herkimer the next morning after the Van der Veers left for home. Emmie and Luke had talked far into the night, and it was decided to try and secure the land on the hill behind the Inn for the new summer home that Charles and Lum wanted to build.

CHAPTER XII

Emmie had no time to be lonesome. Travel on both the canal and overland was heavy and Charlotte, along with Emmie, tended the store, and the O'Donnell and O'Neil children were pressed into service at the Inn.

It was several days before the men returned with papers in hand, allotting Papa 100 acres more or less, which encompassed the whole hill. Luke and the O'Donnell and O'Neil men began almost immediately to mark trees for cutting and clearing a large center section for the building. Plans arrived shortly from New York, and when Emmie saw them, she was stunned. She had envisioned a cabin-like building, but the plans called for what seemed to she and Luke more like a mansion.

More letters with both questions and instructions followed nearly daily. Luke hired several men traveling west who were looking for work, and the path that had led up the hill was widened and the logs from the clearing were fashioned into a roadway. Emmie never ceased to be amazed at Luke's expertise at managing all of the construction that was taking place.

Fall lingered on that year. The harvest was abundant and although everyone was was very busy, they all worked happily together. The vegetables were stored for winter, and many jars of all sorts of preserves lined the pantry at the

Inn. Amid all the hustle and bustle Emmie took Ebony and rode to visit Maria. The foliage was especially beautiful, and the warm fall days made the trip most pleasant, and the news that greeted her was even more so.

Ellen was coming for a visit. She had written to Maria all about Emmie and Luke's visit to the gallery, and had explained as best she could in a letter, about Mr. Wilson's fuss about the painting she had done of the Indian that so resembled Luke. They had settled their differences, and she and Mr. Wilson wanted to visit. She wanted him to get to know her beloved friends as she did. Perhaps they, like the Van der Veers, could have a place nearby, where they could get away from the summer heat of the city.

Emmie was delighted as Maria at the news of the impending visit, and Emmie cut her visit short so that Maria could get on with her preparations.

Back at the Inn more letters and instructions had arrived, and Little Luke and Teka had also arrived and were ready to start their studies. Charlotte took over all the students so that Emmie could spend her time in the store.

The foliage faded, but the warm weather continued. Mr. Wilson and Ellen came, and after the initial greetings, borrowed horses from Luke and rode on to the Swenson farm. On their return trip they were bubbling over with the news that they, too, had decided to return in the spring and secure land for a summer home.

When the frost finally came, it was severe and the canal traffic came to a sudden halt. Some boats were icelocked and the crews looking for winter work and lodging found it at the Inn. No rooms were vacant, and that meant little time for relaxing. Emmie could never remember a winter passing so quickly. Even the children were needed to assist by having regular duties after their classes, leaving little time for skating and sliding.

When the first warm days of spring crept up the valley, the boaters moved on, easing the work at the Inn, but leaving Luke short-handed. His work on the hill had to be finished - getting a cellar dug and a foundation laid. By early May a team of carpenters arrived as well as several large barges with lumber and crates of furnishings, presenting a much bigger problem - they must be stored and protected from the weather, but where? It was Luke who came to the rescue. He directed that tent-like structures, fashioned after Indian tepees, be erected and they worked very well.

The house on the hill progressed rapidly. It was situated so as to look out over the valley. The little settlement could also be seen, but the house could not be seen from the store or Inn. Papa made it clear that he would keep his room at the Inn even after the house was finished. He enjoyed his independence. He spent many days that summer on Emmie's front porch, watching the travelers passing on the canal, and toward Fall he rode down to where his little farm had once been, and had erected a small stone cross in memory of Ma.

The house on the hill began to take shape. The weather for outside work held steady, and before fall, what Emmie had first thought of as a huge monster, began to look more like a castle from a story book. No one visited that summer from New York City. Ellen and Mr. Wilson had changed their plans and had sailed early in the spring for Europe, and both Emmie and Maria had had letters from previously unheard of far away places. Mr. Wilson had sent money to George to secure the property for a new home for them, but with definite instructions that he did not want to locate, even in the summer months, in too remote an area. George and Maria thought that a rather strange request.

In the years since they had staked their homestead, many others had done the same. They had been hours, even days, from neighbors when they first began to build their home and establish their farm. But now there were little settlements all along the banks of the great river, and even up in the foothills of their beloved mountains. Mining camps had sprung up when iron ore had been discovered in the foothills, and logging and lumber camps were many. The building of the canal had brought many migrants from abroad, who, upon completion of the canal, had taken root here in the valley. Little farms were everywhere. Trappers and hunters were vanishing. George felt he would have no problem in securing property for Ellen and her husband.

They had all become quite

fond of Mr. Wilson, but his pompous manner had prevented any of them from becoming familiar enough with him to address him by his given name. Perhaps if he and Ellen spent summers nearby, they would get to know him on more intimate terms.

Once again the harvest season was upon them. Their gardens had flourished, and crops were plentiful. Every corner of storage space was full.

The kitchen at the Inn emitted tantalizing rich aromas of preserves - apple and pear butter, and all sorts of pickles and jams and jellies. Apples were peeled and dried for winter pies. The whole little community was alive with activity. Emmie felt that with the addition of the houses for the O'Donnells and O'Neils, the store house, the school, and now the house on the hill, they were really a budding community.

More crates arrived from New York, and it was decided that the house would be closed in enough so that they could store there. They would also move the crates that had been stored in the tepeelike arrangements since spring to the house on the hill.

With the arrival of the first frost, the carpenters boarded up and weather-proofed the shell of the building, and packed up and took one of the last east-bound packets for Albany. They were sure they could secure work there for the winter, and they would return in the spring to finish the house.

Maria and George arrived for a harvest dinner, bringing with them not only news that George had secured several acres of land for Mr. Wilson and Ellen near the growing community of Deerfield, north of the thriving city of Utica, but also that Ellen would, by Christmas, make them grandparents. They all rejoiced in the news and the women immediately started to make plans for the impending birth. Maria would go to New York to be with Ellen. She would have to travel overland, as the canal would be closed, but her excitement overcame any fears of traveling that she might have.

She and George had come to the Valley as newly-weds many, many years ago. They had been married in their native Sweden, and had immigrated to America. They were both from well to do families, and had used Maria's dowry and George's inheritance to bring them to this new land of great opportunity. They had secured the land where they had built first a crude cabin, and later the house they now occupied. Where the children Jon and Ellen had been born here in the Valley, and George and she had worked side by side over the years to make their little farm a thriving success. George had traveled to the Port of Albany many times over the years to buy and sell and trade for stock and supplies for their farm, but Maria had never been further than the old trading post, and not even there until she had met Emmie on that fateful day long ago when Emmie had come from the mountains in search of a place to sell or trade the furs Luke had accumulated from his trap lines. After their harvest dinner and their rejoicing over all the news that the Swenson's had brought, the little settlement settled down to a quiet fall.

Travel eased off as the weather grew colder. Guests at the Inn were fewer and everyone seemed to have more leisure time. Emmie used her leisure time planning and sewing a layette for the impending birth of Ellen's child. She wanted the gifts ready when Maria left for the city. Luke's interest in her sewing amused her as he was like a child with all his questions as to why and how each finished garment was to be used. Lastly, Emmie used most of the scraps from her scrap-patch basket and fashioned a small quilt. Luke was more delighted with this than any of the other pieces Emmie had made. For this, he said, he could see a genuine use.

The package was ready when Maria and George stopped early in December. George had decided that Jon was capable of tending their farm alone, and so he was going to accompany Maria to the city. They were delighted with Emmie's package, and promised to send news of their arrival at Ellen's, and of the baby's birth. Emmie also entrusted a note to her family with a promise from George and Maria that they would visit them and deliver the note for her.

The news came on the Eve of the new year that Ellen had given birth to twins, a boy and a girl, and everyone in the little valley community was overjoyed.

Mail was very slow in arriving, as overland travel had been

hampered by snow and high winds, and when another letter finally arrived from Maria, Emmie learned that her friends would be staying on in New York City with the Wilson's until spring. Emmie was glad for Maria. The tone of her letter implied that their visit was very enjoyable, and that the babies were growing. She also told of many visits with the Van der Veers, and how she had never imagined, even with Emmie's eloquent descriptions, how these city people lived so lavishly-servants to do even one's slightest bidding.

The elegant dresses that the women wore, and the household appointments bells to summon servants, tubs to bathe in, and carriages to ride in. Even as a young girl in Sweden, Maria could not recall such elegance as was displayed by both the Van der Veers and the Wilsons.

Both George and Maria never ceased to be amazed at how comfortable Ellen was with all this wealth, and with the grace and ease that she greeted notable visitors at the art gallery. As soon as she was well enough after the birth of the twins she could be found painting in her studio.

Nannies had been engaged to care for the children and Maria found that with all of the other household help, she had little to do. George quite often went to the Van der Veer's place of business, and became very interested in the bookprinting and binding business, and on pleasant afternoons Maria visited the many shops in which she never ceased to be amazed. Shops where one could buy but one article? A millinery shop, a shoe shop and a dress shop. There were some stores called department stores, but they were large and confusing for her. There were no shops here like Emmie and Luke's.

On their last evening in the city the Van der Veers entertained George and Maria and Ellen and Mr. Wilson at a lavish dinner. Maria was so taken with all the elegance, that her only thoughts were to try to remember every minute detail to tell Emmie. After dinner they all went to the Opera. Maria was sure she must be in heaven--no place on earth could be as grand as all this.

The winter days dragged on in the Upper Mohawk Valley. The storms seemed more severe than ever, and the winds gusted and whistled around the buildings, making great, nearly impassable drifts of snow. The children were the only ones enjoying this blustery weather. As soon as Charlotte dismissed their classes they would fly past the store with skates flung over their shoulders, and some days not even bothering with their skates and would slide on the canal until supper time.

Luke and the O'Donnell and O'Neil men spent a great many hours clearing paths. They kept two cows and several chickens to supply them with milk, eggs and butter, and their animals had to be tended, the horse stalls cleaned and the horses fed and watered. Water was a problem as the weather worsened, and the well that had been serving them all so well, froze over. The men then had to carry water from the spring on the hill, and quite often, the children were pressed into what they termed "water duty." Taking turns carrying the pails, but sliding down the hill presented many problems in the form of wet, icy clothing, and Emmie voiced her opinion loud and clear that she would be glad to see spring roll up the Mohawk Valley.

March proved to be the very worst time, with the snow banks so high and the winds howling so loud that life seemed unreal. Not one single person passed by all during the month. The banks were so high between the store and house and barn and school and Inn that it seemed almost like walking through tunnels. Emmie wished often that the barn was not so far away, but it had been she who had insisted that it be east of all the other buildings, so as no unpleasant odors might reach the guests at the Inn. Even in the mountains in the little cabin, Emmie could not remember such a winter.

Many evenings they all gathered around the huge fireplace at the Inn and popped corn and drank warm milk, sweetened with maple syrup. Luke often entertained the children with tales of Indian lore and even tales of his experiences after he had married Emmie, and had trap lines to tend, and of how he disliked the White Man's steel traps, and of the baby wild cat he had found that had lost a leg to a steel trap, and was sick and separated from his mother. And how he had brought the tiny animal to Emmie and she had named him Bobby because he had lost not only a leg, but also his tail in the steel trap. And how Emmie had nursed him back to health, and how fast he could scurry around the cabin on three legs. And how finally, one day when Emmie was sweeping and airing out the little cabin, he had rushed out the door and back to his native habitat in the forest.

With these tales and tales from the O'Donnells and O'Neils. how they had helped build the canal, the evenings passed rapidly and March and the storms passed too.

Maria and George arrived on the first packet west. They had ridden from New York to Albany on a steam train.

Maria was so excited, trying to tell Emmie all about the "iron horse" pulling carriages over rails that for the first time since Emmie had known her, she mixed Swedish and English together. Emmie and Luke could not even imagine such a contraption. The rumors that had floated up the valley had been scoffed at as imaginary pipe dreams, but now with Maria and George's revelations, the rumors were a reality.

Emmie called over to the Inn to have some refreshments brought to the porch, and soon the Swenson's were much calmer, and were delivering the rest of their news to Emmie and Luke. They carried a long letter from Charles and Lum with more instructions about the house on the hill. Also, from Charles and Lum, a letter to Papa, which after a short glance, he put it in his waist coat pocket. There was news about Ellen and Mr. Wilson and the babies. The girl had been christened Emmaline, and the boy, Jon, whom Maria already referred to as Little Jon and Baby Emmie.

Mr. Wilson had hired builders from Utica to begin at once on the construction of their home near Deerfield. They felt the twins too young to travel, and so planned to stay in the city for the summer. Emmie and Luke were disappointed at this news as they were both anxious to see not only the twins, but Ellen, too.

The carpenters who had found work in Albany for the winter arrived to complete their work on the house on the hill. And once again the little settlement was alive with activities.

Charlotte dismissed school in May and immediately took over some of the duties of waiting on people at the Inn. It was several weeks before Emmie remembered the letter Maria and George had brought from Charles and Lum to Papa. Papa had never mentioned it, and Emmie hesitated to ask until one evening that was especially warm and humid, they were sitting on the porch watching the lights on the packets and barges that were passing on the canal. They could hear voices and laughter coming from the river, where people were fishing and strolling on the banks.

Papa broke the silence on the porch. He drew out the envelope that he had received from New York many weeks before, and gave it to Emmie. She opened it and read aloud. Chris was going to take over the business in the city. They were selling their home, and would make the move to the Mohawk Valley permanent. And last, but of the greatest significance, they had invested in the Hudson River Railroad Company, and the plans were to extend the railroad not only to Utica, but westward and beyond.

Emmie folded the letter and replaced it in its envelope and returned it to Papa. No one commented. The lights faded on the canal, and the voices quieted along the river banks. The lights dimmed at the Inn, and Papa arose and bid them good night. Emmie and Luke retired shortly. Neither revealing to the other their thoughts.

The sun rose bright and clear and the day's activities proceeded as usual, when with the approach of evening, Luke closed the store and Emmie walked, hand in hand with him, across the lane and took their evening meal at the Inn with Papa as usual. They carried their cups to the front porch of the store, and as the sun faded, they once again watched the traffic on the canal.

Papa was 92 years old, and Emmie was nearing 70. They had lived to see the trails change into highways. The canal had become a reality, and now a railroad was to be built through the valley. A valley, Emmie could no longer think of as her valley, but a valley soon to belong to the world.

As they sat on the porch in silence, a cool breeze came up and Emmie went inside for a shawl. As she returned to the porch and pulled the wrap about her shoulders, and looked out over the valley, her thoughts were years away, when she had run into the hills to escape the horrors of the fire, those many years ago. As far as she could see now, was then wilderness, and when she had returned from the mountains for the first time, several years later, the only persons within miles were the Swensons and the Becker's trading post.

The trail from the Post to the Swenson farm was now only a memory. Just within the last few years, changes had come suddenly and had been drastic indeed. There were man-made roads where the horse paths had been. There were several small farms between their little community and the Swenson's. And on a clear day you could see in either direction, east or west, smoke rising from the smoke stacks of factories in Rome and Utica. And although she and Luke still kept their money in the locked box Mrs. Becker had given them, the travelers had told about banks where they would keep your money safe for you, and also lend you money to build homes and businesses and buy farms.

These communities had become cities and centers of industry. Manufacturers had established textile mills where wide cotton goods were manufactured, and mills where iron and copper was worked. The Phoenix iron works manufactured not only stoves, but Emmie had read, furnaces that one could heat the entire house with a single unit.

Emmie recalled the first time she had seen the iron stove in Mrs. Becker's kitchen, and how amused Luke had been when she had described it to him He had not even been able to imagine such a contraption, and then how proud Ellen had been when she had first cooked on it when she came to live with them at the Post. Surely Charles and Lum would have such a contraption as a furnace installed in the house being built on the hill.

The newspapers from Utica were full of news about an extension, really a separate railroad being proposed. The line was to be called the Utica Schenectady Railroad, and Emmie imagined that some day a railroad would pass their little community.

The intrusion of the canal had been quite silent. The packets and barges drawn by mules had glided silently over the water. The only, and welcome intrusion had been the voices of the canalers and passengers calling out as they passed by. The railroad, as described by George and Maria, was a very noisy contraption. An iron horse emitting great rolls of of smoke and sparks, and the clanking of iron wheels along iron rails. Emmie could not imagine such a machine disturbing the quiet of the valley, but Luke was ecstatic. He wanted to invest as Emmie's brothers had in this new mode of transportation, the machines of the future that would purportedly make them all very rich. Papa, too, was in favor of the railroad, and so it was decided on the first day that the subscription books in the banks were opened to the public in Utica, Luke and Papa rode down to the city and were one of the first investors in the proposed new line.

It was Emmie, not Luke, who could not believe that the official-looking pieces of paper they guarded so secretly on their return, would make them wealthy beyond their imaginations.

As Emmie sat next to Luke that night on the porch, her thoughts were of the changes that he had experienced since they had left his father's compound to follow the ways of Emmie's people. The braid of now graying hair that hung down his back, and the moccasins that he wore while working around their little community were the only visible traits left of the young brave that had rescued her so many years before.

Her thoughts were broken by the approach of men walking up the canal bank from a barge that had docked just below them. It was another load of supplies and furnishings for the nearly finished house on the hill. The men were directed to the Inn for help from the O'Donnells and O'Neils. Papa rose and bid them good night and followed the men to the Inn. Darkness was rapidly engulfing them, and Emmie called to Papa that it would probably be best to have the men put up for the night and unload in the morning.

Just as they were about to retire, the sound of horses hoofs could be heard, and within minutes George and Maria appeared. Luke ran to meet them as they rounded the corner of the store.

Their excitement was evident even before they spoke. They had heard about the public stock subscription for the proposed new railroad, and were on their way to Utica to invest.

Luke and George went inside and Luke showed George the certificate that he was so proud of. Maria, like Emmie, was not as enthusiastic as George was, but was willing to rely on his good judgement.

Emmie and Maria walked in silence to the Inn. They found only Mrs. O'Neil still about, preparing last minute details for the next day's breakfast. She quickly stirred up the dying coals, and set to making coffee for the new arrivals. Luke and George joined them shortly, and they chatted until nearly sun-up, when Luke offered them fresh horses to continue their journey. George and Luke made small talk about travel by horse soon to become obsolete.

As the Swenson's started off for Utica, Luke and Emmie stood and watched them until they were out of sight. Luke took Emmie's hand in his, and neither spoke, but had they confided in each other, they would have been in agreement that not only was their world changing, but the world all around them was changing, too.